Random Thoughts on Love

I Like To Read Something Different To Take A Break From Life

VERONICA ATANANTE KUNG

ReadersMagnet, LLC

Random Thoughts on Love
Copyright © 2021 by Veronica Atanante Kung

Published in the United States of America
ISBN Paperback: 978-1-955603-21-8
ISBN eBook: 978-1-955603-20-1

All rights reserved. No part of this publication may be reproduced, stored in a retrieval system or transmitted in any way by any means, electronic, mechanical, photocopy, recording or otherwise without the prior permission of the author except as provided by USA copyright law.

ReadersMagnet, LLC
10620 Treena Street, Suite 230 | San Diego, California, 92131 USA
1.619.354.2643 | www.readersmagnet.com

Book design copyright © 2021 by ReadersMagnet, LLC. All rights reserved.
Cover design by Ericka Obando
Interior design by Renalie Malinao

CONTENTS

How to use this book vii

Introduction ix

Friday, March 19, 2021 1

Saturday, March 20, 2021 4

Sunday, March 21, 2021 8

Monday, March 22, 2021 10

Tuesday, March 23, 2021 15

Wednesday, March 24, 2021 16

Thursday, March 25, 2021 18

Saturday, March 27, 2021. 20

Sunday (Palm Sunday), March 28, 2021 23

HOW TO USE THIS BOOK

I have read someone write that if I like reading, it is good to spend time reading something I am not likely to read regularly - like the *Smithsonian* or publications of the Humane Society. This book, *Random Thoughts of Love*, is written with this type of reading in mind. Hopefully, you will find it relaxing and a break from life.

INTRODUCTION

I just watched Parousia (Lesson 1) by Scott Hahn. It struck me that he said that all he says is not something he came up with in his imagination and creativity. Nowadays, I find that people are always trying to come up with something new to capture a greater audience. His honesty and humbleness drives me to want to tell you that my writing is not original. Instead it is part of my life to write, in my words, experiences and perspectives from meeting other people.

I focus on continuing to encourage readers suffering from mental illness, anxiety and depression to find their way to reach a relatively happy life by my testimony of my life in writing the book series, *Random Thoughts*.

My books venture into a way of living that makes me relatively happy. This is my way.

This magnified over time making me understand that things are not always black and white. There is grey matter (like in the nervous system).

The **grey matter** throughout the central nervous system enables individuals to control movement, memory, and emotions. Different areas of the **brain** are responsible for various functions, and **grey matter** plays a significant **role** in all aspects of human life.

Like grey matter is in the nervous system, the community of readers with mental illness, anxiety and depression are themselves important. Life would not be life without this community.

So whatever, you are going through - having difficulty in finding the right medication, experiencing loneliness, anxiety and depression and uncontrollable thoughts - I hope you not only find encouragement to make your life relatively happier but also find hope throughout the rest of your life, after reading this book. Through my writing, I depict thoughts that are my testimonies that, with my incurable mental illness, there is hope.

Friday, March 19, 2021

It's 9:24 p.m.

She blessed me and I wrote...

She had asked me why I was upset at her question in the bible study group today. That question raised struck me adversely (as I misunderstood the subject) because it had tampered with my love for the Holy Trinity. Maybe you will better understand my "love" if I gave you this quote from Hannah Whitall Smith (God of All Comfort, page 83),

> *With such a God, who is also a Father, there is no room for anything... When temptations to doubt, or to be anxious and fearful, come to me, I dare not listen to them. To do so would be to cast a doubt on the trustworthiness of my Father in heaven.*

The point is that any question raised in doubt of the Holy Trinity would ultimately cast a doubt on everything God the Father has done in my life. It seems appropriate to go through a list of the things God has done for me, but rather I would like to invite you to think of the things

He has done for you. What blessings have you received? (write down a list of your blessings)

For my blessings, they cannot be defined by a finite number. I am most grateful for Him. But why does He give me these blessings? It can only be described as ABUNDANT LOVE.

How does God give love? In Saint John Paul's apostolic letter, *Salvifici Doloris*, "...the messianic program of Christ, which is at the same time the program of the Kingdom of God, suffering is present in the world in order to release love, in order to give birth to works of love towards neighbor, in order to transform the whole of human civilization into a *civilization of love*."

It's 10:35 p.m.

Made in the Image of GOD

"God created mankind in his image; in the image of God he created them." (Genesis 1:27) So, where Jesus suffered, man will suffer. And, at the same time, where He loves, man will love. Furthermore, when man suffers, God will feel our suffering, Jesus felt our suffering during His time on earth. When man loves, God will feel our love, Jesus felt the love of His Father in His existence on earth. Therefore, if I cast a doubt on God, I will cast a doubt on His love...and the love of the Holy Trinity.

The question raised in the bible study group struck me adversely because of my love of the Holy Trinity. It does not matter what the actual question was because the question was a misunderstanding. However, should I perceive the understanding of future questions on doubting the love of the Holy Trinity, I will be sure to excuse myself.

Saturday, March 20, 2021

It's 8:26 a.m.

ATTITUDE
IS
every
THING

Why do I love? Gratitude. Eve, the first woman, sinned against God. Then God made her female descendants who became mothers who are loved by their children to the moon and back. Is this an inkling of love from God? She SINNED and yet he BREATHED LOVE into her life. I am not here to answer if God has forgiven Eve, but I am here to testify that God gave me my mother who loves me as long as she lives (and inevitably, even after life, I truly believe).

I have a mental disorder which showed its full ugly self when I turned 22 years old. I blamed my mother more than a few times. I hurt her with words. I hurt her with my thoughts. I hurt her with my behavior. Yet, she showed no reproach over the years, just patience and love. Why do I love? I am so grateful God gave me my mother.

She always said to me, "Count your blessings." What is a blessing? was my question the first time I heard this phrase. Then, I learned. My blessing is in my relationships, my blessing is my daughter; my blessing is my husband; my blessings are my siblings; my blessings are my parents; and, my blessings are people around me.

My mother had managed to spread her love and patience to everyone. This I learnt from her and I was able to spread it to others - other members of the family and friends. God created Eve, the first woman, to shine as a temple of His love up to this day. That is why I love.

There is another kind of love - love of all in nature and all in art (including music and literary arts). Everything in nature shows the peace and beauty of God. It begins with the creation of the world in the book of Genesis,

> Then God said: Let there be light, and there was light. (Genesis 1:3)

> Then God said: Let there be a dome in the middle of the waters, to separate one body of water from the other. (Genesis 1:6)

Then God said: Let the water under the sky gather into a single basin, so that the dry land may appear. (Genesis1:9)

Then God said: Let the earth bring forth vegetation: every kind of plant that bears seed and every kind of fruit tree on earth that bears fruit with its seed in it. (Genesis 1:11)

Then God said: Let there be lights in the dome of the sky, to separate day from night. Let them mark the seasons, the days and the years, and serve as lights in the dome of the sky, to illuminate the earth. (Genesis 1:14-15)

Then God said: Let the water teem with an abundance of living creatures, and on the earth let birds fly beneath the dome of the sky. (Genesis 1:20)

Then God said: Let the earth bring forth every kind of living creature: tame animals, crawling things, and every kind of wild animal. (Genesis 1:24)

Man, in his creation in the media, cannot omit nature and art. These creations can be seen on our cellphones constantly. The account *Sealegacy,* in Instagram, uses a combination of beautiful pictures/videos and music and words, involving land and sea creatures, to raise the awareness of protecting the earth that many love to the core of their heart. The website *Only One*, creates nature videos and nature stories which appeal to those people that have a love for the earth (God created). The music composer *Ludovico Einaudi*, creates music of his love in the observation of nature.

If anyone happens to come across these types of creation, how can anyone not have this kind of love stir up in them? This love is full in God's creation of the world. A world of love can be a civilization of love, filled with kindness and compassion. Consequently, creating a world with a sense of peace and beauty.

I need only to concentrate on love such as this.

> *What consumes your mind, controls your life.*

Sunday, March 21, 2021

It's 8:16 a.m.

Love such as this, has no hidden agenda. Love is a gift and here is a little story.

Two weeks ago, I was suffering from anxiety. It felt like this time, it is the worst it has ever been and there is no cure. Darkness engulfed me and I had trouble breathing. I begged silently to know why I am suffering. I thought in err that God is not around. Just as I thought, I had reached my end, my Lord and my God prompted my husband to pray over me. I came out of it, victorious with only one word in mind.

"One word

[Frees us of all the weight and pain of life:]

That word is love." ~ Sophocles

This was God's love manifested in my husband's action. He felt my suffering and gave the grace of prayer to cast out the evil spirits like the way demons were casted out in the bible. God gave this as a gift. That is, He does not expect anything back for His conscience or possession.

I understand that it is human nature to give and want to receive something back - bartering! Even giving and wanting to please one's conscience is bartering, in a sense. God gives love as a gift (not asking for anything back).

Monday, March 22, 2021

It's 12:59 p.m.

About God's love, I contemplated on the Shroud of Turin while watching the Virtual Tour of the Exhibition - WHO IS THE MAN OF THE SHROUD. (Without the help of music and visuals here in my writing, the words below are still excruciatingly painful for me).

The shroud showed a man with wounds in his head. I know from scripture; Jesus wore a crown of thorns. It's His way of saying,

> "I am the sin bearer. The sins of all the world are laid upon me. I bear them in my passion." (WHO IS THE MAN OF THE SHROUD - Virtual Tour of the Exhibition)

As the soldiers laid him on the cross, I imagined,

> "With His hand stretched at 90 degrees and then he is hoisted up. Plopped down on top of a vertical beam which is already standing planted in the ground and now

> His arms sag some 25 degrees and all the weight of His body is hanging on the two nails. And, it is not until the third nail is placed through both feet. . ." (WHO IS THE MAN OF THE SHROUD - Virtual Tour of the Exhibition)

He dies, again imagining,

> "On His right side, between the 5th and 6th ribs, penetrates a roman lance. . .[pause] a wound of about 4 centimeters with a double edged blade gives kind of an almond shaped wound. This is a distance of about 3.5 inches to the heart." (WHO IS THE MAN OF THE SHROUD - Virtual Tour of the Exhibition)

These are pains that only God's love can bear.

ONE DAY YOUR PAIN WILL BECOME THE SOURCE OF YOUR STRENGHT.

It's 2:12 p.m.

The last time I was suffering from anxiety, my husband prayed over me. God gave him the grace of prayer to rid me of my terrible thoughts. Last night's suffering was different. I received the grace of wisdom where a little voice made a simple advice, "Love Yourself."

you're a limited edition

I was in a state of dissolution that everything was something to worry about. I worried about my computer crashing. I worried about my child. I worried that my memory failing. Everything under the sky worried me. Then, that little voice said, "Don't be so hard on yourself. You don't have to think so hard." Then, "love yourself."

Many times I have heard this from other people. But this time, I needed to just do that. But, again like peace (in my blog), I did not know what that meant. So, I asked my daughter and she answered, "Don't hate yourself." That made it click in my head. It meant no anger and frustration towards myself; no lies to put into my head which lead me away from God; and no laziness. It meant, when I come face to face with God on judgement day, I would be able to sincerely answer His question, "What did you do with the life I gave you?" In other words, God gave me life and at the end, there is inevitable death. But what is the story in between?

The Best Way to Predict the Future Is to Create It

It's 2:42 p.m.

In my story, love begins at home. Although this is common, I feel the need to share with those that suffer from mental illness, anxiety and depression, and are in a family or will be having a family.

When Eve sinned in the book of Genesis, God still breathed love into the life of a woman. I believe this same love was breathed into my role as a mother.

At the beginning when my daughter came into this world, I made a vow to willingly give my time to her. I wanted to make sure she knew what the love God breathed into me meant for our family. There were times in the middle of the nights she woke and cried. Despite being tired, I would wake up and cradle her. Every day I would make sure she had enough milk. No matter how busy I was, I would make sure I gave her my full attention to play with her. When she got older, I got busier with life and still made sure I would listen to her stories daily.

When she came from school broken, I was there to hug her. When mathematics class became difficult, I spent time working problems out with her. When the pandemic began, distance learning started and she became my prime focus. What was most important to her was that I took time with her for everything.

I truly believe to give my time to my daughter was what God made me for. This is the type of home my own mother perfected for me for many years.

Tuesday, March 23, 2021

It's 3:10 p.m.

I love my guardian angel. Like in the old cartoons with a small devil on one shoulder and a small angel on the other shoulder, the angel has a task of shepherding, guarding and to provide light for me. The guardian angel is a creation of God and as God is love, it follows that the guardian angel disseminates love and belongs to the order of good. So, I speak to God every night to give extra strength to my angel. (Don't ask about the devil on the other shoulder! ☺)

It's 3:33 p.m.

God is eternal love. (Pints of Aquinas video on The Conversion of Dr. Scott Hahn) For me, this is a state of peace, happiness, warmth, coziness, abundance, goodness, kindness, trust, humility and eternal life. Rightly so that Job 10:12 says, "Life and love you granted me, and your providence has preserved my spirit."

Wednesday, March 24, 2021

It's 7:17 p.m.

Love the poor. I was about to enter the freeway 10. The traffic light was red. I saw a homeless person standing on the pavement by the red light. My heart shatters to see the homeless. So, I rolled down the window and grabbed a handful of change (all I had) to give to this person. He came up close and received then he growled and through the handful of change over the bridge into the freeway. I was frightened. Then, the light changed and I drove onto the freeway.

Another time, I was taking public transportation. I got on the bus and sat at the front by a mostly empty bus. I sat in the same row with space between a homeless person and me. That person reached out and touched me on my shoulder. I was frightened. Then, the bus reached my destination and I got off the bus.

Yet another time, I got off at a bus stop and there was a homeless person. As I waited to cross the road, the person came closer to me and touched me indecently. I was frightened. I shouted at him and hurriedly crossed the road.

God says, "Blessed are the poor in spirit, for theirs is the kingdom of heaven." Was God talking about the homeless persons I met? Perhaps. But more importantly, I think he was speaking to me.

Being frightened, I did not want to have anything to do with the poor again. My heart would beat at a high rate at every encounter. My fear made me step back and away from the poor. After many years, in the company of good people, I grew to set aside my fear and have thoughts of compassionate connections for the poor. My experiences and my mental illness became secondary. Now, I saw that perhaps the homeless person just needed something to eat or to drink, or just needed to talk. I dream of owning a home open to the homeless community. The times a homeless person approached me now, I felt a sense of patience. I would watch documentaries of nurses giving their time to treat the homeless of ailments by administering medicine to them, for free. I would make it a point to support initiatives that home the homeless. Although, at times I have also learnt to look away, the fact is that I cannot help everybody. But I have begun spending time praying for the homeless. Perhaps praying seems to be a small unimportant task to some but I am encouraged by good friends who believe in God that prayer is essential. God gave me strength in prayer and kept my fear aside. As St Therese, the Little Flower said, do the little things with great love.

Thursday, March 25, 2021

It's 6:26 a.m.

". . .the light shines in the darkness, and the darkness has not overcome it." (John 1:5)

"For God so loved the world that he gave his only Son, so that everyone who believes in him might not perish but might have eternal life." (John 3:16)

Some of my favorite verses in the bible (do you have a couple of favorite quotes?).

Love is a light. It cannot be lukewarm. It is hot like fire. No matter how I think of it, it cannot be extinguished by anything that is dark. They say God is Love. They also say God, the Holy Spirit and the Son are one. It follows that the Son is also love and cannot be extinguished by darkness. That is why there is the resurrection.

It's 5:33 p.m.

Love transformed me. Everyday I would tell my family that I loved them before they told me. It is very important to take the initiative on expressing love to your family - to give love is to receive love.

Saturday, March 27, 2021.

It's 9:04 a.m.

This morning I explored and have decided to go off topic and narrate a dream I had. This is part of an experiment in my writing. In my mental illness, I have relative happiness in life because I have chosen to experiment and be creative with my ability to write. Writing may be of interest to my reader or not, but it is of interest to me.

I had a dream. I couldn't take it anymore. This was sexual harassment. They would kiss behind his car on the other side of the road in front of everyone. They had no shame that they were married to their spouses.

I was feeling unwell as these things always made me feel unwell. So, I was scheduled to work with Tung in the front desk all day. I decided that I would work with my likable boss for 8 hours instead. I spoke to her, "Since I am not feeling too well today, I thought that I would work with you and speak to Tung that I am working with you today." I had wanted to work with my female boss because I liked dancing (my job) more than working in the kitchen (my other job). My boss agreed.

I spoke to Tung and it was already past 9 o'clock - the start time. He was quietly and nicely telling me off that I was late. We were in the front desk, too. The electronic billboard was already up telling the guests that I would receive their registration forms. My name was flashing in the billboard. Then, I told Tung that I was not well and had talked to my female boss that I would be working with her. He was disappointed for a short while because he had looked forward to working with me. He had taken a liking to me. Anyway, he asked the male receptionist behind the concierge desk if he was busy. Fortunately, he said no. I was covered.

I went back to my female boss to report for work and found out that I would be attending the front desk too. My female boss sat me down in the back office and two women came into the room. She said, "Too bad. . .we have to fill out the forms again!" I began filling up forms that had been filled out yesterday by the two women and worked until 6 p.m.

I came out after finishing the last form and met the bus boy who had worked in my absence. He was admiring one of the dishes on one of his registration forms a guest had filled out as his signature dish. I talked for a while but got distracted by my female boss going over to the other side of the room. I politely excused myself and walked towards her.

As I drew closer, I noticed Mary and Hannah were there with my boss. They had laid out stacks of letters around them, on the floor and the seats. There was work to be done. Mary was stuffing envelopes. She said to me, "Can you help us?" I answered cheerfully as a joke,

"Mary, every time I see you, you are asking me to work?" Although I had joked, Mary took it seriously because she never got my jokes. I was bad at telling jokes - bad deliverance, I guess. I said, "You know I was joking, only to make you happy that I see you again. . ." I worked.

Sunday (Palm Sunday), March 28, 2021
It's 8:46 a.m.

I longed to go to 9 a.m. Mass this morning just to acknowledge to God that I know He loves me. I asked my daughter last night if she would go with me. I mentioned to my husband it was Palm Sunday with the hope that he would skip his weekly bike ride to go to church with me. The answer from both was not a resounding no but a response that they would rather go about their business.

My daughter slept in. My husband went on his bike trip. These were not dissimilar to how Jesus was welcomed into Jerusalem with people singing, "Hosanna!", then being crucified by the end of the week. YET, Jesus continued His path to the crucifixion. Why? I believe it is because He loved mankind or humankind. In the bible, it says,

> "For God so loved the world that He gave his only Son." (John 3:16)

What is this love? I have written about love but have not written about the purpose of love? This is a mystery to me, especially why God so loved the world. Perhaps there is something good about mankind or humankind, that God sees in the world. In any case, I want this love and I pray it grows.

This may be an awkward way to close; to leave a reader dangling but I write to make the reader contemplate about love in his or her own life and I encourage this to be done in silence.

For me, this is Palm Sunday and although I will not make it to church, I will wake up my daughter and take a walk, and attempt to contemplate God's meaning of love.

Before ending this book though, I must add that despite our choices on Palm Sunday, I do not doubt God's love for us - only He can exude that kind of love.

love your life

www.ingramcontent.com/pod-product-compliance
Lightning Source LLC
LaVergne TN
LVHW021049100526
838202LV00079B/5412